AUG 1 2 2021

THE FLYTRAP FILES

By TOM ANGLEBERGER

Illustrated by

HEATHER FOX

DJ Funkyfoot #1

Butler for Hire!

Amulet Books · New York

PUBLISHER'S NOTE: This is a work of fiction. Names, characters, places, and incidents are either the product of the author's imagination or used fictitiously, and any resemblance to actual persons, living or dead, business establishments, events, or locales is entirely coincidental.

Cataloging-in-Publication Data has been applied for and may be obtained from the Library of Congress.

ISBN 978-1-4197-4728-1

Text copyright © 2021 Tom Angleberger
Illustrations copyright © 2021 Heather Fox
Book design by Heather Kelly

Published in 2021 by Amulet Books, an imprint of ABRAMS. All rights reserved. No portion of this book may be reproduced, stored in a retrieval system, or transmitted in any form or by any means, mechanical, electronic, photocopying, recording, or otherwise, without written permission from the publisher.

Printed and bound in U.S.A.
10 9 8 7 6 5 4 3 2 1

Amulet Books are available at special discounts when purchased in quantity for premiums and promotions as well as fundraising or educational use. Special editions can also be created to specification. For details, contact specialsales@abramsbooks.com or the address below.

Amulet Books® is a registered trademark of Harry N. Abrams, Inc.

ABRAMS The Art of Books
195 Broadway, New York, NY 10007
abramsbooks.com

To Brook Bibb —T.A.

CONTENTS

Opening

 y phone rang.

"Greetings," I said. "I am DJ Funkyfoot, and I am at YOUR service."

"Good," said a prickly voice. "I'm Cactus Kwame of Cactus Kwame's Roller Rink and Disco Rodeo. I need a DJ for our big Disco Rodeo Roller Boogie Contest tonight!"

"Ah," I said. "I'm afraid you have made a common mistake, sir."

"No way!" said Cactus Kwame, and he was extra prickly. "I never make a mistake."

"Yes, sir," I replied, even though I knew he HAD made a mistake. I am a butler who serves tea, not a DJ who plays music.

"So can you come over and play us some crazy disco beats tonight or not?"

"I'm afraid not, sir," I said. "As I was trying to tell you: I am not a DJ."

"Whoa! Hold up! Aren't you DJ Funkyfoot?"

"Yes, sir."

"But you're telling me you're not a DJ?"

"No, sir," I said.

"Then why do you call yourself DJ Funkyfoot?!" yelled Cactus Kwame.

I did not yell back. I remained calm. I have had a lot of training to become a

butler, and part of that training is not getting mad.

"My parents named me DJ Funkyfoot because they hoped that I would someday become a hip-hop star."

"Well?" asked Cactus Kwame. "Did you become a hip-hop star or not?"

"No, sir," I said, "I became a butler."

"A butler?"

"Yes, sir."

"What does a butler do?"

"I do whatever my employer needs me to do," I said. "For example, I might prepare a cup of tea in the early evening."

"I don't want a cup of tea in the early evening!" yelled Cactus Kwame. "I want crazy disco beats all night long!"

"I don't do that."

"But it'll be on TV! I thought you hip-hop stars loved to be on TV!"

"I'M NOT A HIP-HOP STAR! I'M A BUTLER!"

"Well, you must not be a very good one if you go around yelling at people like that!"

He was right! I had forgotten my training! I wasn't being a good butler!

"I am so sorry, sir," I said, but Cactus Kwame had hung up.

PART 1

....

Butler
for Hire!

Chapter 1

My phone rang.

"Greetings," I said, reminding myself to be polite no matter what the other person said. "I am DJ Funkyfoot, and I am at YOUR service."

"Great!" said a stressed-out voice. "We want to hire you!"

"Very good, ma'am," I said. "But before you hire me, I must make sure you know that I am not a hip-hop star."

"Why would I want to hire a hip-hop star?" asked the stressed-out voice.

"I don't know, ma'am," I said, "but many people do and—"

The stressed-out voice interrupted me.

"I don't need to hire a hip-hop star. I need to hire a nanny!"

"I'm sorry, ma'am, but I am not a nanny either."

"What are you?"

"A butler, ma'am."

"That's close enough!" yelled the stressed-out voice. "We can't afford to be picky. Another nanny just quit on us! That makes forty-three! And you're the only nanny I can find."

I had to remember my politeness training.

"Again, ma'am, I am a butler, not a nanny."

"Who cares? It's the same thing!"

"Excuse me, ma'am, but a nanny and a butler are not the same thing. In fact, there are some very important differences to—"

The stressed-out voice interrupted me again.

"I don't have time to quibble!" yelled the stressed-out voice. "Get over to Murky Pond Park right now!"

The stressed-out voice hung up.

Chapter 2

was happy.

I was happy even though I had been yelled at and hung up on twice in one morning.

I was happy because I was going to have a job again.

I needed a job REALLY bad!

You see, I used to be the butler for a very rich poodle named Countess Zuzu Poodle-oo.

However, she invested all of her money in a robot that made cookies. When the robot went crazy and destroyed the city, she lost all of her money.

So I lost my job.

I was very sad when I lost my job. So I called my mother.

"You should have listened to us and become a hip-hop star," said my mother. "You know, it's not too late! Let me sign you up for breakdancing lessons!"

But I did not want breakdancing lessons. And I did not want to be a hip-hop star. And I did not want to play crazy disco beats all night long. I wanted to be a butler!

I had worked hard to become a butler. Years of study. Years of training. Years of working as a page, then a footman, then a valet, and finally . . . a butler.

I'll never forget the first time I put on my butler's uniform: a scratchy shirt with a stiff collar, a hard-to-tie tie, and a long coat with tails that kept getting stuck in doors and toilets.

And now I was going to put that uniform on again! I was going to live my dream again! I was going to butle!

So I was happy . . . although I was also a little concerned, since the stressed-out lady said she really wanted a nanny. There are important differences between a nanny and a butler.

But since I needed a job really really bad, I didn't have time to quibble.

I did take the time to have a bath, comb my tail, and put on my uniform. A butler needs to look and smell good at all times.

And then I headed for Murky Pond Park.

Chapter 3

I stepped outside and waved for a cab.

One zoomed up and screeched to a stop on the sidewalk right in front of me. The driver was Countess Zuzu Poodle-oo.

"Yo, DJ FF," said Countess Zuzu Poodle-oo.

"Good morning, Countess," I said. "I am, as always, at your service."

"Naw, it's the other way around now," said the Countess. "I'm here to serve *you.*

I traded in my limo for this cab, and now I'm a taxi driver."

"But Countess," I said, "you don't know how to drive!"

"That's true," said the Countess. "In fact, it might be best if you drove."

She slid over, and I climbed in and drove myself to Murky Pond Park.

"That'll be fourteen dollars," she said. "Plus tip!"

I paid, got out, and looked around the park for my new employer.

It was a lovely park with a murky brown pond surrounded by beautiful trees and shrubs.

"Hold that cab!" an oak tree yelled at me.

"We're late to catch a train!" an elm tree yelled at me. I recognized the elm tree's voice! It was the stressed-out lady who wanted to hire me.

"Greetings," I said. "I am DJ Funkyfoot, and I am at your service."

"You're hired," said the oak tree.

"We'll be back by midnight," said the elm tree. "Take good care of ShrubBaby!"

As a butler, part of my job is to never act surprised or say "WHUT?"

Unfortunately, this time it slipped out.

"WHUT?"

"I said take good care of our daughter, ShrubBaby, the Adorable Baby Shrub. That's your job. You're ShrubBaby's new nanny."

"I am a butler, ma'am."

"Butler, nanny, whatever," said the stressed-out elm tree as she squeezed into the taxi. "We don't have time to argue with you. Just take care of our adorable baby shrub!"

"Cabbie! Get us to the train station! FAST!" yelled the oak tree as he squeezed into the taxi, too.

"WAIT!" I called. "I'm not sure you understand the very important differences between a nanny and a butler!"

But the Countess stomped on the gas, and the taxi roared off in a cloud of dust and falling leaves.

I was left standing in the middle of the park, next to a small shrub.

"Hi," said the small shrub.

Interlude

S o," said the small shrub. "What is the very important difference between a nanny and a butler?"

"Well," I said, "a nanny's job is to say no. A butler's job is to say yes."

"I don't get it," said the small shrub.

"A nanny's job is to be wise and wonderful and to help a child grow up safe and sound. This may require the nanny to tell a child no or even 'Absolutely not!'"

"Sounds awful," said the small shrub. "What about a butler?"

"Well," I said, "a butler's job is to do whatever they are asked. This may require them to say, 'Yes, ma'am' or 'Absolutely, sir.'"

"Sounds a lot better," said the small shrub. "Can you give me an example?"

"Certainly," I said. I looked around the park and saw a pickle relish truck not far from the pond.

"Here is an example. Imagine that a child said, 'I want to drive that pickle relish truck into that pond.'"

"OK. I am imagining that."

"Well," I said, "the nanny would say, 'Absolutely not,' and the butler would say, 'Very good, miss, I will go find the keys.'"

"Thank you," said the small shrub. "That was a very good example."

"You're very welcome," I said. "Now I think I had better find ShrubBaby, the Adorable Baby Shrub."

"I am ShrubBaby, the Adorable Baby Shrub," said the small shrub.

"I am DJ Funkyfoot, and I am at your service."

"Good," said the adorable baby shrub. "Because I want to drive that pickle relish truck into that pond!"

"Very good, miss. I will go find the keys," I said.

PART 2

A Star Is Sprouted!

Chapter 4

I ran thirteen blocks carrying the adorable shrub!

I wanted to get away from the park before the pickle truck's owner showed up. I had read the name on the side of the truck: COUSIN YUK YUK'S PICKLE RELISH!

That Cousin Yuk Yuk is a scary guy! And he gets very angry when anyone messes with even one jar of his pickle relish. So I did not want to be anywhere near the park when he found out that an entire truck-load had been spilled into the pond.

But after running thirteen blocks, I just had to stop. I was tired, soaking wet, smelling like pickle relish, and carrying a surprisingly heavy adorable shrub.

"That was fun!" said ShrubBaby.

"I disagree," I said. "If I was a nanny, I would tell you what a terrible thing that was to do and put you in time-out for the rest of the day."

"Good thing you're not a nanny," said ShrubBaby.

I started to get mad, and then I remembered that nannies sometimes get mad (in a nice way), but butlers never do.

Also, ShrubBaby, the Adorable Baby Shrub was such an adorable baby shrub it was hard to get mad at her.

"You must admit," I said, "that driving a pickle truck into a pond is not all that adorable."

"Who wants to be adorable?"

"I thought you did, miss."

"No!" she shrieked. "That's just what my parents want."

"Ah," I said. "My parents want me to be a hip-hop star, not a butler. So I can understand that, miss."

"Why do you keep calling me 'miss'?"

"Well, that is a title often given to young ladies."

"I don't like it," said ShrubBaby. "What else you got?"

"Ahem, well . . ." I said, thinking. "Many butlers say 'Yes, my lady' or even 'Yes, m'lady.'"

"Oh, that's better," she said. "You may call me 'M'Lady ShrubBaby.'"

"Yes, M'Lady ShrubBaby."

"Now, the next thing I want to do is . . . watch TV!"

ShrubBaby pointed at a store window. Inside, a gigantic TV was showing some kind of game show starring a very tall turtle.

"Yes, M'Lady ShrubBaby," I said.

We went into the store. It was Dougie Bug's ShrubBuggies and Too-Wide Widescreen TVs.

I set ShrubBaby down in front of the TV.

A very handsome spider came over to see me.

"Hey and howdy! I'm Dougie Bug," said Dougie Bug. "You look like you need a ShrubBuggy . . . and a towel."

He handed me a towel.

"Thank you," I said, and did my best to remove as much pond water and pickle relish from my fur as I could. However, I was unable to remove the smell of the pickle relish. "Please excuse my odor, sir."

"No problem," said Dougie Bug. "I smell using my legs, so I'll just be sure not to kick you. Ha ha. That's just a little spider humor. Now, would you like to see our ShrubBuggies?"

"Yes, please. That little shrub is heavier than she looks."

Dougie Bug showed me a beautiful buggy with eight wheels, air-conditioning, cupholders, a stereo, and a widescreen TV that seemed a little too wide.

"This is our best buggy," he said. "You and your adorable baby shrub will be able to see the whole city in style and comfort!"

"How much does it cost?" I asked.

"A million dollars."

I reached into my pocket and pulled out a damp five-dollar bill. It was all the money I had left!

"Do you have anything that costs five dollars?"

"I can let you have this used ShrubSnuggly for $4.95," said Dougie Bug. He held up a big tangle of straps.

"What's a ShrubSnuggly?" I asked.

"It's like a backpack, but you wear it on your front so your shrub can see where you're going."

"What about style and comfort?" I asked.

"Nope," said Dougie Bug. "You'll look like a fool and it will be extremely uncomfortable."

"The show's over," said ShrubBaby. "I want to go! And I want to see where I'm going!"

"Yes, M'Lady ShrubBaby," I said.

I gave Dougie Bug my five-dollar bill. As soon as he touched it, he said, "Ugh, this money smells like pickle relish!"

Then I put on the ShrubSnuggly and loaded up ShrubBaby.

I looked like a fool and was extremely uncomfortable.

ShrubBaby still looked adorable, of course.

"Let's go!"

"Yes, M'Lady ShrubBaby."

Chapter 5

ome back when you're ready to buy a way-too-large television!" called Dougie Bug as we stepped outside.

As soon as the door closed behind us, I heard a familiar voice.

"Aha! There they are!"

It was Inspector Flytrap. He's a Venus flytrap plant that solves crimes. He gets around on a skateboard with the help of his partner, Nina the Goat. She's a goat.

"I've solved the Mystery of the Pickle Relish in the Pond!" shouted Inspector Flytrap.

"Big Spill," muttered Nina.

"Oh dear . . ." I said.

"We followed the wet pawprints all the way from the park," said Flytrap. "Even I, one of the world's two greatest detectives, am surprised to find out that it's you, DJ Funkyfoot!"

"Butler did it," said Nina.

"But it wasn't me," I said. "It was—"

But I stopped myself just in time! I couldn't tell them it was ShrubBaby! I was supposed to be taking care of her, not tattling on her to the World's Greatest Detectives. What could I do?

"Run!" squealed ShrubBaby.

"Yes, M'Lady ShrubBaby!!!" I said. And I did! As fast as I could!

But Nina started pushing Inspector Flytrap's skateboard after us!

We ran down streets and up alleys. We ran under a cow on a ladder, dodged a kiwi driving a truck, jumped over three porcupines fixing potholes, scrambled through a presidential parade, and slid under a very tall turtle.

"That was very impressive," said the very tall turtle as we ran past. "You'd be great on my TV show!"

"STOP!" yelled ShrubBaby.

"Yes, M'Lady ShrubBaby," I said, stopping. "But may I point out that we are being chased by the World's Greatest Detectives?"

"No problem there," said the very tall turtle. "One of the World's Greatest Detectives stopped to eat a parade float!"

I looked behind us. A block away, I could see Nina the Goat on top of a parade float chewing a bunch of flowers while both Inspector Flytrap and President Horse G. Horse yelled at her.

"Whew, thanks," I said to the turtle.

"You're Very Tall Turtle, the host of the show I was just watching!" yelled ShrubBaby.

"That's right," said Very Tall Turtle.

"And I was just on my way to the studio to film the next episode! You and your nanny should be on my show."

"Actually, I'm not a nanny, I'm—"

"Yes!" yelled ShrubBaby. "That is what I want! I want to be on TV!"

"Yes, M'Lady ShrubBaby," I said, and we followed the very tall turtle into the TV studio.

"What's the name of this show?" I asked.

"*Ultimate Disaster Masters Showdown: Extreme*," said Very Tall Turtle.

"Oh dear," I said.

Chapter 6

Very Tall Turtle led us to an elevator.

DIRECTORY

FLOOR 1
Lobby

FLOOR 4
Name That Name

FLOOR 2
Ultimate Disaster Masters
Showdown: EXTREME

FLOOR 5
Kissy-Kissy Time!

FLOOR 3
Extreme Cake Bakers
Showdown: ULTIMATE

ROOF
Penguini's Rooftop
Restaurant

"We film different game shows on every floor in this building," he said. *Ultimate Disaster Masters Showdown: Extreme* is on the second floor."

The elevator doors opened, and I saw a wild and crazy jungle gym. Ladders and ramps and ropes and steps and slides and swinging sofas and tiny ledges were all suspended over a giant pool of water.

"Oh dear," I said.

"WHOO-HOO!" yelled ShrubBaby. "Let's rock and roll!"

"Yes, M'Lady ShrubBaby."

"I've got to go up to the announcer's booth," said Very Tall Turtle. "You two go ahead and get in line."

There was a line of five very strong-

START

looking animals and one rutabaga with huge muscles.

"Hey," said the rutabaga. "Isn't this awesome?"

"Yes," said ShrubBaby "It's totally awesome."

I was too frightened to say anything other than "Oh dear."

One by one, the others ran, swung, and jumped through the crazy course while Very Tall Turtle yelled a lot.

"That was an incredible run by Rutabaga Annie. She wins fifty thousand dollars! Next up, we have a team:

DJ Funkyfoot and ShrubBaby, the Adorable Baby Shrub! Ready! Set! Go!"

"Oh dear," I said. "I cannot do any of that!"

"I thought you had to do whatever I asked?"

"But some things are impossible."

"But what if I ask you to do it anyway?"

Very Tall Turtle interrupted, "The clock is ticking! You're running out of time!"

"But listen—"

"Are you a butler or a nanny?" asked ShrubBaby.

"A butler, of course," I said.

"THEN GO!!!!!!!!!!" yelled ShrubBaby.

"Yes, M'Lady ShrubBaby!"

I ran toward the first obstacle: a thirty-foot jump over a pool of water to grab a rope to swing over another pool to grab a bar to flip up and over a rolling log and land on a plastic duck suspended over a firepit.

"Now they're moving!" said Very Tall Turtle. "Let's see if this hip-hop star can jump as well as he can rap."

"Ah," I called back, "I'm afraid you have made a common mistake—"

"LOOK OUT!" yelled ShrubBaby.

"Yes, M'Lady ShrubBabeeeeeeee-eeeeeeeeeee!"

I missed the end of the ramp, and we both fell a long long way into the water. But it wasn't water! It was sticky, sweet red soda.

"Uh-oh," Very Tall Turtle said. "Looks like they fell into the Dippy Doo Dunk Tank, sponsored by Dippy Doo Beet Soda, a division of Yuk Yuk Industries."

As I staggered out of the pool carrying ShrubBaby, I heard Very Tall Turtle saying, "Well, that 'raps' things up for the hip-hop star and the incredibly adorable baby shrub! They didn't win any money, but they will get a coupon for a free lunch at Penguini's Rooftop Restaurant."

Interlude

We took the elevator up to Penguini's Rooftop Restaurant.

"Ah! Welcome, my friends," said a well-dressed penguin. "You look like you could use some lasagna, some mulch, and . . . some towels."

He showed us to a table and ran off to get our lunch.

I unstrapped the ShrubSnuggly and let ShrubBaby sit in a booster seat.

Then I sank into my chair. I was exhausted, wet, and sticky, and I smelled like both pickle relish AND sugary beet soda.

"That was incredible!" squealed Shrub-Baby. "I'm going to be on TV! In fact, I'm on TV right now!"

ShrubBaby pointed to a TV hanging on the restaurant wall.

The show was on.

And we were on the show. They were airing an instant replay of our huge splash into the red soda.

Then the TV started to show a commercial for toenail fungus, and I lost my appetite for the lasagna.

PART 3
....
Fame and Misfortune
(and Slime and Kissing)!

Chapter 7

Well," I said to ShrubBaby, "I'm glad that I was able to be of service and help you get on TV. Now perhaps it is time for a nap . . ."

"A nap?!" yelled ShrubBaby, with her mouth full of mulch. "Didn't you hear the turtle? There's a different show on every floor of this building!"

"But surely now that you've been on TV—" I began.

"I want to be on TV more!" finished ShrubBaby. "Now that I've tasted the glory of being on TV, I won't stop until I'm famous!"

"But—"

"Nope," said ShrubBaby. "No nanny talk."

"Yes, M'Lady ShrubBaby."

We thanked Penguini, gave him the free-lunch coupon, and then returned to the elevator.

"Ooh! Ooh!" squealed ShrubBaby, adorably. "Let's do the cake baking show."

"Yes, M'Lady ShrubBaby," I said.

I don't know how to bake a cake, but I was relieved that she hadn't asked for the *Kissy-Kissy Time!* show. I saw that on television once, and there was a lot of kissing! That's even worse than being covered in pickle relish and sticky beet soda!

We took the elevator to the third floor.

DIRECTORY

OOR 1

F   2

FLOOR 4
Name That Name

FLOOR 5
kissy-kissy Time!

ROOF
Penguini's Rooftop Restaurant

Chapter 8

The show's studio looked like a giant kitchen, but it was full of chickens with cameras and microphones.

One enormous chicken came running over to us.

"I'm Little Red Hen, the host of this show. One of our contestants just quit, and we need a new one. Who will help me? Who will be on my show?"

"We will!" hollered ShrubBaby.

"One moment," I said "Would you please tell us why the other contestant quit?"

"He thought it was too dangerous," said Little Red Hen. "Now put on these hats, and let's start baking!"

The hen pushed us into the middle of the kitchen. A dinosaur and a camel were already standing there with chef's hats on.

"3, 2, 1 . . . We're on the air!" shouted a chicken with a camera.

"Welcome to *Extreme Cake Bakers Showdown: Ultimate!*" clucked Little Red Hen. "Today we have the country's best bakers taking on our toughest challenge yet: the world's tallest wedding cake!"

Chickens started hauling out huge pans, big bags of flour, barrels of frosting, and fifty-two-foot-tall ladders.

"Our contestants today are the best of the best. Jacques Raptor from Paris, Datrice the Camel from Rome, and . . . what was your name again?"

"I'm ShrubBaby and this is my butler, DJ Funkyfoot!"

"Wow, an adorable shrub and a hip-hop star!" clucked Little Red Hen.

"That's a common mista—"

"Sorry, hip-hop star, there's no time for chitchat. You only have twenty-two minutes to bake your cake. Starting . . . NOW!"

It ended badly.

We raced for the elevator with Little Red Hen, Jacques, and Datrice chasing after us.

We jumped in, and the door closed just as Datrice was about to bonk me on the head with an eggbeater!

Now I was covered in smelly pickle relish, sticky red soda, AND gloopy, drippy cake frosting! With sprinkles!!!

"I'm sure you'll want to return home for a bath and a nap," I said, hopefully. "Right?"

"Stop talking like a nanny and push the button for another floor!"

Only my years of butler training stopped me from yelling, "NOOOOOOOOOOO!"

Instead, I said, "Yes, M'Lady Shrub-Baby," and pushed the button for floor 4.

Name That Name didn't sound THAT bad, and at least it wasn't *Kissy-Kissy Time!*

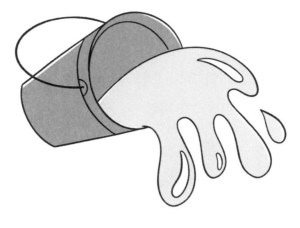

Chapter 9

inutes later we were sitting in a little booth with a microphone.

Madame Mushroom was asking us questions.

I had gotten nine right so far, and a sign made out of lightbulbs was flashing: $9,999.

"Alright," said Madame Mushroom. "Name one more name, and you win ten thousand dollars. Make a mistake, and you lose it all and get covered in twenty thousand gallons of slime."

"WAIT! WHAT?" I yelled, forgetting to talk like a butler for a second. "You never said anything about slime!!!!!!"

"That's the name of the game," said Madame Mushroom.

"I thought the name of the game was *Name That Name*?"

"Oh yeah, I forgot," said Madame Mushroom. "There's so much slime, I just assumed it was in the name. It smells really bad, too. They should add that to the name. Hey, Tiffany, can we change it to *Name That Name or Get Covered in Stink Slime*?"

"NO!" yelled a walrus wearing a headset and a hula skirt.

"Sorry, Tiffany says no," said Madame Mushroom. "Anyway, are you ready for the final question?"

"YES!!!!!" squealed ShrubBaby.

"Before I ask the final question, let me just say what a pleasure it has been to have an adorable baby shrub and a hip-hop star on our show today. Aren't they great, folks?"

The audience of five hundred hamsters applauded wildly.

"BA-BY SHRUB! HIP-HOP STAR!" they chanted while stomping their tiny feet. "BA-BY SHRUB! HIP-HOP STAR!"

"That's a common—" I began.

"Shhh . . . total silence, please, as I read the final question . . ." said the mushroom.

The hamsters got quiet. ShrubBaby and I got quiet. Madame Mushroom got quiet.

We sat there for a long time.

Finally, Madame Mushroom whispered.

"For ten thousand dollars, what is the

name of the famous painter who painted the *Mona Spaghetti*?"

I knew the answer, of course, since I'd seen that painting at the museum many times. But before I could answer—

ShrubBaby squealed, "Vacuum cleaner!"

"That was adorable!" gushed Madame Mushroom. "But wrong."

Madame Mushroom pushed a button, and I heard the sound of gears turning, motors roaring to life, liquid sloshing. High overhead, an enormous tube popped out of the ceiling, and . . .

I'd really rather not talk about it.

Roll, Baby, Roll!

Chapter 10

I staggered back to the elevator covered in smelly pickle relish, sticky red soda, gloopy icing (with sprinkles), and a thick coating of slime!

"And now . . . time for the *Kissy-Kissy* show!" squealed ShrubBaby.

"No . . . Please . . . Not that . . . Just let us go home," I begged.

"That doesn't sound like butler talk," said ShrubBaby. "It doesn't even sound like nanny talk."

"It's not," I groaned. "I'm not asking you as your butler or your nanny . . . I'm just asking as a dog covered in sticky, smelly, disgusting glop . . . please please please please let us go home."

"But I want to be on TV!" squealed ShrubBaby.

"Yes, M'Lady ShrubBaby," I said and pushed the button for floor 5.

Chapter 11

The elevator doors opened.

The first thing we saw was a pair of giant neon lips blowing neon kisses.

It was all dark, except for a spotlight that was shining on a very handsome elk. The elk was wearing a purple tuxedo and holding a bouquet of roses. He was singing the show's theme song:

Kissy ... Kissy ...

Kissy ... Kissy ...

Kisseeeeeeeeeeeeeeeeeeeeeeeeeeeeeeeeeee eeeeeeeeeeeeeeeeeeeeee Time!

"Thanks, everybody! I'm Very Handsome Elk, the host of *Kissy-Kissy Time!* And now, get ready to meet tonight's Kissy-Kissable contestants—they're . . . totally adorable!"

A spotlight swung over to shine right in our faces.

An enormous crowd starting cheering and yelling.

"So adorable!"

"Totally adorable!"

"I've never seen such an adorable shrub!!!"

Suddenly, all the lights came on.

We could see the audience for the first time.

It was all trees.

Trees of all shapes and sizes and leaf colors, but they all had one thing in common. They all thought ShrubBaby was adorable.

"LET THE KISSY-KISSY KISSING BEGIN!!!!!!!" yelled Very Handsome Elk.

"Get me out of here!" squealed Shrub-Baby.

"Yes, M'Lady ShrubBaby."

Chapter 12

We ran out of the studio.

I pushed the elevator button, but before the doors opened, all the trees came stomping out of the studio.

"SO ADORABLE!"

"SO KISSABLE!!!!!!!"

"DON'T LET IT GET AWAY!!!"

"Those trees are going to smother me with love!" screamed ShrubBaby. "Head for the stairs!"

"Yes, M'Lady ShrubBaby!"

I ran for the stairs. The trees stomped after us!

"Slide down the bannister!" yelled ShrubBaby.

"Yes, M'Lady ShrubBaby!"

I slid down the bannister, but the trees all did, too! And as we passed the third floor, a door flew open!

"They're getting away!" yelled the dinosaur and the camel wearing chef's hats.

"NOOOOOOOOOO!" yelled the walrus with the hula skirt, jumping on the bannister, too.

We finally hit the ground floor, and I sprinted for the door!

As soon as we got outside, I heard a familiar voice.

"AHA!" yelled the familiar voice. "I have found the criminals!"

I looked up the street. There was Inspector Flytrap on his skateboard with Nina the Goat pushing him. And with them was Cousin Yuk Yuk himself!

"Aha!" yelled Flytrap. "There they are!"

"NOW I WILL CLOBBER THEM!" yelled Cousin Yuk Yuk.

I turned to go back inside, but now the trees were stomping out the door.

"There's that adorable little shrub," they bellowed.

"RUN!" yelled ShrubBaby.

"Yes, M'Lady ShrubBaby."

I ran, but, of course, so did the four

hundred love-crazed trees, the dinosaur and camel wearing chef's hats, the walrus in a hula skirt, Nina pushing Flytrap, and Cousin Yuk Yuk.

"MUST CLOBBER!" yelled Cousin Yuk Yuk.

"MUST KISS!" yelled the trees.

"Must run faster!" yelled ShrubBaby. "They're gaining on us!"

"I'm sorry . . . I can't, M'Lady Shrub-Baby! I yelled. "The frosting has started to dry out! I can barely move my legs!"

I was slowing down! Everybody else was speeding up!

Suddenly, a taxicab zoomed by.

"Need a lift?" It was Countess Zuzu Poodle-oo.

I dove in through an open window!

"Get us out of here!" squealed Shrub-Baby.

The Countess stomped on the gas, and the taxi shot forward.

We left all of them behind in a cloud of dust.

"NOOOOOOO!" We could hear Cousin Yuk Yuk and the trees yelling as we zoomed around a corner on two wheels.

"Thank you so much for the rescue, Countess," I said. "But please drive safely!"

"Pretty please!" added ShrubBaby.

"Don't worry," said Countess Zuzu Poodle-oo. "I've been driving all day and have only had three accidents so far. That's my personal record!"

"Then may I suggest turning the wheel sharply to the left?" I said.

The Countess turned the wheel just in time, and we did not run into the miniature golf course!

Instead we ran into a fountain with a statue of President Horse G. Horse.

Don't worry, no one was injured (except the statue).

Epilogue

The fountain began to wash away the layers of slime, frosting, and pickle relish. And I started to feel better.

But ShrubBaby started to feel worse.

"I'm so sorry," she whimpered.

And then she started to cry in the most adorable way ever.

"A-boo-hoo-hoo. A-boo-hoo-hoo-hoo."

I gave her a hankie.

"No offense, but this hankie is super gross," she said. "Most of the slime and frosting has washed off, but it still smells like pickle relish."

But then she blew her nose in it anyway.

"I think . . . I think maybe I asked for too much," ShrubBaby sobbed.

"Yes, you did," I agreed.

"I guess I got what I deserved," said ShrubBaby. "I wanted to be on TV, but now I wish I hadn't. Instead of being famous, I looked like a fool."

"I'm afraid so," I agreed.

"And I made you look foolish, too. I bet butlers don't like to look foolish."

"No," I agreed, "we don't."

"All I really wanted was a chance to show everybody that I'm more than just an adorable baby shrub! I wanted someone to think I was awesome, not just adorable."

"I understand, ShrubBaby," I said.

"You do?"

"Yes," I said. "I have the same problem. It can be hard to get people to see the real you."

"Yeah," she sniffed.

"But I'm not so sure that TV shows are the best place for that," I said.

"Well," said ShrubBaby, "at least not THOSE TV shows. I need to find one that lets me show my true talent."

"What exactly is your true talent?" I asked.

"Roller disco," said ShrubBaby.

"Pardon me," I said. "I need to make a phone call."

I got out my phone. Luckily the water-proof case was also slime-, frosting-, and pickle-proof.

"Hello, Cactus Kwame? This is DJ Funkyfoot. Do you still need a DJ to play crazy disco beats for you tonight?"

"You bet your roller boots I do!" Cactus Kwame shouted back at me.

"Great. I'll be right over."

"I knew I was right about you!" hollered Cactus Kwame. "I told you I never make mistakes! Now get on over here, the TV cameras are ready to roll."

"That's great," I said, "because I'll be bringing a very awesome, not-just-adorable baby shrub with me, and she is ready to roller boogie. Isn't that right, ShrubBaby?"

"Yes, DJ Funkyfoot, I am."

ABOUT THE
AUTHOR AND ILLUSTRATOR

TOM ANGLEBERGER is the *New York Times* bestselling author of the Origami Yoda series, as well as many other books for kids. He created DJ Funkyfoot, a Chihuahua butler, with his wife, Cece Bell, for the Inspector Flytrap series. In real life, Tom and Cece do have a Chihuahua, but he's more of a biter than a butler. Visit Tom at origamiyoda.com.

HEATHER FOX is an illustrator of stories for children. When she isn't creating, she's probably drinking a hot cup of coffee, eating Chinese food, or chasing down her dog, Sir Hugo, who has stolen one of her socks. She lives in Lancaster, Pennsylvania, with her husband (and author!) Jonathan Stutzman.